CW00841639

Dedicated to Sophie

CHARLIE'S HIGH ADVENTURE

Reprinted 2005

CHAPTER 1

A NOISE FROM ABOVE

Very early one morning, whilst everyone in the jungle was still fast asleep, there came a strange sound.

It was a sound that had not been heard in the jungle before. It woke up the insects who started humming in tune to its strange vibrating tone.

It woke up the birds that started chattering to each other with their secret calls that only they understood.

It woke up the big cats and soon their terrifying roars announced that they were angry at being woken so early from their slumber. In fact it wasn't long before the whole jungle was wide-awake.

Then, the strange sound that was responsible for all the commotion — slowly — faded away.

The loud drone of the insects melted into a quiet hum.

The chattering from the birds became a whisper.

The big cats stretched and yawned as they lay back down to sleep and for a moment it seemed as though peace and harmony had returned to the inhabitants of the jungle.

But suddenly, the strange sound returned, this time much louder than before.

Whatever it was that was making the strange noise and disturbing the early morning peace of the jungle was, at that moment, a mystery. But whatever it was — it was getting louder and louder — and closer and closer — to a little pair of dark round sleepy eyes that all of a sudden opened wide and glared all around.

"What's that noise?" said Charlie as he jumped out of bed.

"Yes what can it be?" said Charlie's father, as he woke half startled by all the excitement.

"Where do you think it's coming from?" said Charlie's mum.

"We don't know!" came the reply, as the two males rushed to look out of the window.

"It seems to be coming from above the trees but I can't see anything," said Charlie's father.

"Do you think there's a storm approaching dear?"

"It doesn't sound like a storm to me. Perhaps it's a monster that eats little chimps," joked Charlie's father.

"Maybe it's a flying saucer," said Charlie pulling his T-shirt over his head and dressing as fast as he could.

"And where, young man, do you think you're going in such a hurry?" inquired Charlie's mum.

"I'm going to find out what's making that noise," replied the little chimp.

"Not until you've eaten breakfast and brushed your —."

But before Charlie's mum could say another word, the little chimp had jumped to his feet and was heading for the door.

"Come back at once!" yelled Charlie's father, "there could be danger out there."

"Wait, come back!" called his mum.

But the mischievous little chimp was fast off the mark; he could not wait to discover what the strange sound was, or where it was coming from.

All his thoughts where focused on finding the strange whirring noise that had invaded the privacy of his jungle home.

His little heart raced with excitement as to what he might find and on his swift little legs he quickly disappeared into the — dense — dark — jungle.

"I'd better go after him at once," said Charlie's father, "there's no telling what's out there.

Without doubt, it's the strangest sound I've ever heard. Let's hope that it's not a monster that eats little chimps."

"Oh dear!" sighed Charlie's mum.

"Oh dear indeed!" sighed Charlie's father, as they both gazed anxiously out of the window.

CHAPTER 2

LITTLE BOY LOST

Driven by his excitement the little chimp had not heeded the warnings his parents had given him. Quite the opposite. In fact, he'd taken it upon himself to find the strange sound and to discover just what it was that was making it. He had, without even thinking about it, made it his task and his task alone, to discover the source of the strange vibrating sound that had startled him out of his sleep only a few minutes ago. But brave as he was, it suddenly dawned on our little hero that he had travelled a long way from the safety of his treetop home. As Charlie began to realise this, the sound that he was so anxious to find was suddenly right above his head and very, very loud.

Birds flew, screeching from their nests in the high treetops to escape the strange whirring sound. Little animals scurried quickly away to the safety of their hiding places. Leaves and branches came tumbling down as dust from the ground swirled up into the air.

All of a sudden the little chimp began to feel afraid.

"Oh my goodness!" he cried as the sound got louder still.

Charlie felt as if the sky was about to fall on his head.

"Help!" he cried at the top of his voice, "help — help!"

At that moment Charlie wished he'd listened to his parents as they had called for him to wait, but it was too late now and he felt sure something terrible was about to happen. His little body began to shake with fear. He put his hands over his ears and closed his eyes tight as he crouched to the ground. He hoped the dreadful sound would go away so that he could go home. Never had the little chimp felt so afraid. Then amidst all the noise and commotion he heard a familiar voice.

"Charlie, over here — are you alright?"

Still trembling, Charlie opened one eye and peeped through his little dark fingers.

"Father it's you!"

"Are you alright my boy?" called Charlie's father, as he raced towards his son.

"Yes father," replied the frightened little chimp, putting on a brave face.

"Thank goodness you're safe my boy. I was so worried."

Just then, in a small grassy clearing only a short distance from where the two chimps were standing, came a sight that Charlie would never forget. A strange machine descended slowly out of the sky and touched gently down in the long grass. Charlie watched in amazement.

"Why — it's a helicopter Charlie. That's what's been making all that noise; it's nothing to be afraid of," said Charlie's father in a much-relieved voice.

As the helicopter landed the pilot turned off the engine. Almost instantly the noisy machine that had scared poor Charlie out of his wits became very quiet.

Whoosh —— whoosh —— whoosh, came the sound as the rotor blades slowly ground to a halt.

Leaves and branches came tumbling down as dust from the ground swirled up into the air.

The doors of the helicopter opened and out stepped two men. They both looked very worried.

"Can you help us?" asked the pilot.

"What's wrong?" replied Charlie's father.

"We have a little boy lost — in the jungle," said the pilot. "He wandered off last night, and we've been searching for him since daybreak. This is Mr Rodgers the boy's father. He's very worried. Please can you help?"

"What's the boy's name?" asked Charlie.

"His name is Tommy," said the boy's father, "he's four years old. I'm here to take photographs for a magazine, that's my job," explained Mr Rodgers, "I brought Tommy along because I thought he would enjoy the trip.

Then, last night while I was preparing supper at our camp he just disappeared. I searched and searched but there was no sign of him anywhere."

"The jungle here is so dense — we can't spot him from the air, we need a ground search," said the pilot.

Suddenly the little chimp that had been so afraid only a few minutes ago, had now forgotten his fears.

Rescuing the missing boy was now his top priority.

"Don't worry Mr Rodgers — I'll find Tommy," said Charlie.

"I'll start looking right away."

And before anyone could say another word the little chimp scampered away.

"I'll find Tommy, Mr Rodgers — leave it to me!"
"Charlie wait — come back — don't you dare run off
again!" cried Charlie's father at the top of his voice.
But in the time that it takes a happy dog to wag its tail our
little hero had once more disappeared out of sight.
"Oh dear!" said the pilot.
"Oh dear indeed!" said Charlie's father.

Charlie watched in amazement.

CHAPTER 3

GUESS WHO TAKES THE PLUNGE

Eager to find the missing boy, Charlie had once again taken matters into his own hands. Not having learnt from his recent experiences the headstrong little chimp found himself once more alone in strange territory.

His intentions were of the best. He only wanted to find Tommy and return him safely to his worried father. But as he scrambled and swung through thickly wooded trees he once again felt a chill of fear as time and again he came face to face with residents of the jungle he'd not met before. Both he and they showed their surprise at their unexpected meetings, with loud screeches and lots of arm waving as they almost clashed into each other.

But the determined little chimp carried on. No one would have thought any less of our little hero had he not gone on alone. In fact his father would have been much relieved to see that cheeky little face return safely.

In Charlie's mind, however, there lingered only one thought.

He was going to be the one to find Tommy.

How pleased everyone would be when Charlie returned with the missing infant. He could almost see the look on their faces. "Well done," they would say and how proud his father would be. But first he had to find the missing boy.

"Tommy, where are you?" Charlie called at the top of his voice, "Are you there — where are you?"

Time and again the little chimp called out but there was no answer. Deeper and deeper into the jungle searched our little hero his alert eyes searching everywhere for the missing child.

But there was no sign of Tommy.

Feeling a little weary Charlie stopped for a moment to catch his breath. He breathed a deep sigh as he looked anxiously around.

"Oh Tommy, where can you be?" whispered Charlie to himself.

The tired little chimp sat for a while listening carefully to the familiar sounds of the jungle. He could hear running water ahead and decided it was time to quench his thirst. The fast flowing stream looked cool and Charlie was very hot. He took a tight hold on a large overhanging branch whilst he drank. All of a sudden there was a huge splash as a large stone hit the water soaking our little hero from head to foot. The sudden shock made Charlie lose his grip and he plunged headfirst into the cold rushing stream.

"Bah — bah!" screeched the little chimp as he scrambled and clawed his way out.

"Got yaa!" came a cry from above.

"Ha, ha, ha, — got yaa!"

Charlie knew that voice well. It was Jeremy, Charlie's cousin.

"What are you doing here?" said the little chimp, shaking off the cold water.

"I came to see what you are up to," replied Jeremy, still giggling, "did you enjoy your bath?"

"Oh very funny — I don't think — and how, may I ask did you find me?"

"That was easy," boasted Jeremy, " I could hear you shouting for Tommy."

"Then you know about the missing boy."

"Indeed," said Jeremy, "I bumped into your father — he told me the whole story, he's not very pleased about you running off on your own."

"No time for that now," exclaimed Charlie, "we've got to find Tommy before any harm comes to him."

"Then may I suggest," said Jeremy with an air of authority, "that we start looking in the right place."

"And I suppose you — know where he is," said the little chimp, in a very sarcastic tone.

"Well if my calculations are correct and providing he hasn't been eaten by a lion, or swallowed by a snake, we should find him somewhere about here," said Jeremy, drawing a map with his finger in the soft earth.

"Then there's no time to lose — come on Jeremy, let's go!"

"Err — wouldn't you like to take another bath before we leave?"

"Don't push it Jeremy!" said the little chimp as once more he set off on his quest to find the missing boy.

"Wait for me!" called Jeremy.

But Charlie had set off as though he'd been fired from a cannon.

"Charlie wait — wait for me!"

But in the time it took Jeremy to find his feet, Charlie had yet again disappeared into the dark — leafy — surroundings.

"Oh dear!" said Jeremy.

He plunged headfirst into the cold rushing stream.

CHAPTER 4

IN THE NICK OF TIME

"Why doesn't someone teach that chimp some manners?" muttered Jeremy, as he trundled along in search of his cousin. "Doesn't he know it's not polite to run off and leave his best friend like that, especially when that best friend came to help. After all, had it not been for me, he wouldn't have had his bath." Jeremy giggled to himself at the thought of Charlie falling into the cold water. "Serves him right — that'll teach him — the impatient little —."

But before Jeremy could think or mutter another word, a terrifying cry broke the silence and echoed all around. Jeremy felt a cold shiver run down his spine.

"What on earth was that?"

The eerie cry had stopped Jeremy in his tracks.

Did a certain little chimp have anything to do with that dreadful noise, he wondered?

Instead of feeling bitter about Charlie's disappearing act Jeremy now feared for the safety of his little cousin.

Quickening his pace, and moving swiftly on, Jeremy called out.

"Charlie it's me, Jeremy — can you hear me? — Charlie it's me —."

"Up here!" came a reply.

Jeremy looked up and there, on one of the tallest branches overhanging a stony ridge, was the little chimp.

"Quick Jeremy — up here — as quick as you can — come on, hurry!"

Jeremy scaled the tall tree as fast as he could leaping from branch to branch. In no time at all he'd joined his cousin, in the high swaying treetop.

"Look!" said Charlie, "over there, on that rock."

Jeremy looked to where his cousin was pointing. A tall jagged rock stood some twenty or so metres above the sharp stony floor, and there on it's tiny ledge, clinging on for dear life, was the missing boy.

"That's got to be Tommy," said Jeremy, "but how on earth did he get on there?"

"He must have stumbled off that ledge in the dark. Poor little fellow must have been there all night."

"If he falls from there, he's —."

"That's not the only problem," interrupted Charlie, "take a look over there."

Jeremy's eyes followed Charlie's finger once more as he pointed to an old broken tree that had fallen, making a bridge across the high rocky gorge.

There, perched on its dead branches, were a pair of the ugliest most ferocious looking birds you can imagine, their huge heads bowed, and their wings poised, ready to strike at the helpless little infant.

"Oh no!" said Jeremy, as he breathed a deep sigh, "vultures."

"I'm afraid so," said Charlie, "I got here in the nick of time. They've attacked once but I hit one of them with a stone. It gave out such a screech as it flew off."

"So that's what I heard," said Jeremy.

"But how are we going to get Tommy off that ledge? We'd have to grow wings and fly, to get him off there."

"That's it Jeremy, that's the answer!"

"It is?" said Jeremy, looking a little puzzled.

"Hold the fort Jeremy, I'll be back as fast as I can. Hold on Tommy, help's on its way!"

Charlie scrambled down the tree as if his own life depended on it.

"Keep those devil birds at bay Jeremy — till I get back — throw anything at them."

"I'll do my best Charlie."

But even as Jeremy spoke, the huge birds where spreading their wings, ready for action.

"Oh dear!" muttered Jeremy.

CHAPTER 5

TWO LITTLE HEROES

Jeremy steadied himself in the upper branches of the tall tree. Armed with only a few stones he prepared to defend the little boy from the menacing buzzards.

"Hold on Tommy, help's on its way!" called out Jeremy, trying to reassure the little chap that everything would be all right. "Can you hear me Tommy? Help's on its way!"

But the little boy said nothing he just lay there clinging with all his might to the jagged rock.

Then with its huge wings spread, one of the monstrous birds launched itself into the air and swooped down towards the stranded child. Jeremy took careful aim, "Here we go!" he cried, as he hurled the first stone at its flying target. The huge bird screeched with pain as the stone struck its bony head.

"Bulls eye!" shouted Jeremy, "one down and one to go." Following its partner the second bird joined the attack, its large glassy eyes fixed on the helpless little boy but Jeremy's aim was true and a sharp stone thudded as it found its target. Again and again Jeremy fought off the attacking birds as they swooped and dived in an effort to make a meal of the stranded little infant, their razor sharp talons striking at the child with every pass.

But breathless and growing tired and with only one stone left in his armoury Jeremy felt the battle was being lost.

"I can't hold them off much longer — if help doesn't arrive soon —- its going to be all over for Tommy."

With an eerie cry the evil looking birds launched themselves once more into the attack.

Jeremy knew he had to make his last shot count.

The tired little chimp gave it everything he had.

"Take that!" he cried, as he hurled the stone with one last mighty effort. A second later, and with an ear -piercing - screech, one of the buzzards tumbled out of the air and crashed to the rocky floor.

"Got yer!" cried Jeremy.

But his joy turned quickly to fear as he looked down on the stranded child. The other giant bird was about to snatch up the little boy in its huge talons and Jeremy could do nothing to help.

"Get away — leave him alone you horrible beast!" screamed Jeremy.

But the monstrous bird was inches away from making a kill. Jeremy couldn't bear to watch. With his heart pounding and his body shaking he turned away, listening for the cry that would tell him that it was all over for Tommy. Then suddenly from out of the sky, came a whoosh — whoosh — whoosh sound, followed by a huge blast of wind that almost blew Jeremy out of the tree, as the helicopter passed low overhead.

"There he is Mr Rodgers — down on that ledge!" said the pilot, "there's Tommy."

Without a moment to spare, the helicopter pilot instinctively turned his machine and dived straight for the attacking bird. The buzzard screeched with fright as the noisy helicopter passed inches over its head.

Blown around in the huge downdraft the hungry scavenger had lost its meal. But one pass from the helicopter was enough, for the monstrous bird wasted no time in making its escape.

"Hooray — hooray!" cried Jeremy.

As the helicopter came to a steady hover, a breathless little chimp arrived on the scene.

Jeremy scrambled down the tree and hugged his cousin.

"He's safe Charlie, Tommy's safe, the helicopter got here just in time."

"Then all we have to do is get him off that ledge. I have an idea," said Charlie.

"Can you hear me?" shouted the little chimp, waving his arms at the helicopter.

"Only just," replied the pilot.

"Have you got a rope?" screamed Charlie at the top of his voice.

The helicopter pilot nodded, he'd grasped the idea without Charlie having to say another word. Mr Rodgers made safe one end of the rope and threw the other end to the waiting chimps below.

"Tie it round my waist Jeremy — good and tight now."
Charlie grasped the rope in his right hand, he took a deep
breath, then signalled to the pilot that he was ready.
The helicopter started to climb and our little hero was
hoisted high into the air.
"Careful," said Jeremy.
Charlie had never been so far away from the ground. It was
one thing swinging in the high branches but dangling on the
end of a rope hung from a helicopter was something else.
The pilot brought the helicopter to a halt over the jagged
rock and very slowly began lowering the little chimp down
towards the stranded infant.
"Tommy give me your hand — come on Tommy — reach
out to me!" called Charlie.
The little boy looked up and Charlie could see that he was
very frightened.
"It's no good — I can't reach him!"
Jeremy signalled to the pilot to lower Charlie just a little
more, but as he did the rope started to swing and Charlie
found himself almost clashing into the sides of the rocky
gorge.
"Come on Tommy you've got to help me!" screamed
Charlie. But Tommy had a clam like grip on the rocky
ledge and was going nowhere. Jeremy could see that all
was not going to plan, the pilot was struggling to hold
Charlie as he dangled on the end of the rope and the little
boy was either too weak or too scared to move.

Something had to be done and done quickly.
(Who knows, when in times of desperation, what spurs one into action?)
Without a moment's thought Jeremy picked a stone from the ground and hurled it at Tommy.
"Get up!" he cried, "move yourself!"
The little boy instinctively sat up and yelped as the stone struck him hard.
It was enough for Charlie and he grabbed the little fellow by the hand.
"He's got him — he's got him!" cried Jeremy, waving frantically to the pilot.
Charlie clung to the shivering little infant with his last ounce of strength as they twisted and swayed on the end of the rope. The pilot moved them as gently as he could, and it was a much relieved Jeremy who reached out and pulled the pair to safety,
"You're alright now Tommy, you're safe," said Jeremy, as he untied the rope from his little cousin.
"Well done Charlie."
"Well done yourself," said Charlie and for a brief moment the two chimps stared at each other and the smile on their faces needed no explanation.
"Come on Tommy," said Jeremy, "time to go home."
The little boy tried to get to his feet, but he was so weak, he just toppled over.
"Oh dear!" said Charlie.

Charlie clung to the shivering little boy
with his last ounce of strength.

CHAPTER 6

CHARLIE'S REWARD

Charlie had signalled to the pilot that they would meet at the clearing where the helicopter could land.
"Ever played piggyback Tommy?" asked Charlie.
The little boy nodded.
"We'll take it in turns Jeremy — lend a hand."
Tired and weary from their ordeal the two little chimps somehow found the strength to carry the shivering infant back to safety.
"Tommy — oh Tommy!" cried Mr Rodgers, as he ran to meet the trio.
The little boy burst into tears as he saw his father.
"Daddy — daddy!" he cried.
Mr Rodgers scooped the little boy into his arms and held him tight.
"I'll never let you out of my sight again — ever!"
"Thank you — thank you for saving my son's life," said the boy's father, smiling at the little chimps.
"How can I ever repay you?"
"I - think - I - know - how," said the pilot, as he arrived on the scene, "but first we had better get Tommy to a doctor. Charlie, your parents are waiting — over by the helicopter."
"Now you're for it," said Jeremy.

"Thanks a bunch," groaned the little chimp, as he dragged himself off to face the music.

"Now then, you pair of scoundrels," said Charlie's father.

"But father —."

"And who was told not to run off on his own?" said Charlie's mum, sternly.

"But mother —."

"And you're just as bad Jeremy, you should have known better. Whatever will your mum say?"

Charlie's parents went on for what seemed an eternity.

"I have only one more thing to say," said Charlie's father. "Well done my boy — well done Jeremy."

There was just enough time for smiles all around before the helicopter whisked Mr Rodgers and Tommy high into the sky.

"Well, I suppose we'd better head for home," said the little chimp.

"Have some refreshments first," said Charlie's father, "your mother has brought them along specially."

"Yes dear, you must be hungry and Jeremy looks absolutely starved," said Charlie's mum, winking to her husband.

"What's going on?" asked Charlie.

"You'll see soon enough. In the meantime sit and refresh yourselves."

Jeremy and Charlie did just that; they had sandwiches and buns and lemonade.

"This is as good as a birthday party," said Jeremy, "In fact it's better than —."

"Shush — listen," said the little chimp, "do you hear it?"

"It — it's the helicopter — it's coming back." said Jeremy. The pilot landed the helicopter in the long grass, just as he'd done earlier that same day.

"Tommy's fine," he announced, as he stepped down from his machine.

"Just a few cuts and bruises — doc says he'll be as right as ninepence in a day or two."

"That's wonderful news," said Charlie's mum.

"Indeed it is," added Charlie's father.

"But had it not been for Charlie and Jeremy — well — things could have been a lot worse — yes, they certainly deserve their reward," said the pilot.

"Reward?" said the little chimp.

"I take it your mum's not told you yet — well," said the pilot, "to say thank you for rescuing Tommy, Mr Rodgers has bought two tickets for a helicopter ride for two very-special little boys.

Well what are you waiting for?" said the pilot.

"You mean us?" said Jeremy.

"Do you see any other little boys around?" asked the pilot.

"Oh my!" said Charlie.

The two chimps climbed into the helicopter and were soon having a wonderful time as they flew high above the treetops.

"Look — down there — that's your house Jeremy — look, your mum's waving."

"Over there Charlie — there's your house."

"Doesn't the jungle look beautiful from up here?" said Charlie.

The pilot flew the two little heroes over the rocky gorge, where they had rescued Tommy.

"Oh my goodness," said Charlie, "it all looks so wonderful from up here — you will remember to thank Mr Rodgers for us."

The helicopter swooped and dived and the little chimps loved every minute.

But like all good things, it was all over too soon.

Having said their goodbyes once back on the ground, it was time to call it a day and head for home.

"Come on little fellows, time to go," said Charlie's mum. "We'll drop Jeremy off on the way."

That night, a little pair of dark round eyes were shut tight as one weary little chimp fell fast asleep.

"What a day!" said Charlie's mum.

"You can say that again."

Charlie's mum smiled, "well, at least they both enjoyed the helicopter ride,"

"Yes, Charlie said that he enjoyed it so much that when he gets up in the morning he's going to build his very own flying machine."

The parents looked deep into each other's eyes and several moments of silence passed between them.
"Oh dear!" said Charlie's mum.
"Oh dear indeed!" said Charlie's father.

THE END

*The helicopter swooped and dived
and the little chimps loved every minute.*

'Charlie And The Hidden Treasure Of Umbahroo'

The second book in the series.

Charlie finds himself in deep trouble as he goes in search of a legendary hidden treasure. There's lots of fun and frolics along the way. And with Charlie in charge of proceedings what could possibly go wrong?

Charlie And The Curse of Zandra

The magical third book in the series.

"Great powers of Tokem — heed Zandra's call — let this chimp grow very small." but no one believes in that hocus - pocus —— do they?

'Charlie's Alpine Adventure

The forth book in the series.

The chimps win a competition and find themselves on the ski slopes of snowy Austria. Charlie, quite by accident, makes an enemy of a certain old gentleman and the fun really begins.

Why not visit Charlie on his website **www.charliethechimp.com** or email him on **info@charliethechimp.com**

The 'Charlie the Chimp' Series is published by: **FLINTON PRESS.**
17 Ullswater Drive, Gillshill Road, Kingston Upon Hull HU8 0JZ. (England)

PRINTED IN ENGLAND BY:
Fisk Printers Ltd. Lee Smith Street, Hedon Road, Kingston Upon Hull HU9 1SD